To
Eloise

# I Dreamt I Was A Princess

Written By Keith Lawrence Roman

Illustrated By Barbara Litwiniec

*I Dreamt I Was A Princess*
*Morningside Books Softcover Edition*
*Copyright © 2013 Keith Lawrence Roman*
*All rights reserved.*
*Published in the United States of America by*
*Morningside Books, Orlando, Florida*

*This edition is cataloged as:*
*ISBN 978-0-9827288-8-8*
*MorningsideBooks.net*

*Printed in the United States of America*

# I Dreamt I Was A Princess

Other girls might play with dolls or like to shop for clothes.
Most people call them girly girls, - I'm not one of those.
I like a ribbon in my hair, and dress in pink not blue.
But when it comes to play and fun I've other things to do.

I'm not afraid of holding frogs, or mud splashed on my shoes.
And I've been known from time to time to climb a tree or two.
My mom says I'm a tomboy, but I would disagree.
Whether in a dress or jeans, I'll always be just me.

On my walls are pictures of places far away.
Of castles tall and ladies all dressed up in silk and lace.

You wouldn't ever know it by looking at my face,
That I've a secret wish to be a lady filled with grace.

When I go to bed at night, I close my eyes and see,
A fairy tale set long ago that features little me.

I dreamt I was a princess dressed in silk and lace.

And everyone who knew me said "She has exquisite taste."
"Was there ever ever a lovelier young lass?"
"Did any princess ever have a quarter of her class?"

In my princess dream, I was the fairest of the fair.
I wore a ball gown every day, and wore it everywhere.

My rainy days were filled with games like tossing rings or queek.

And when the sun was shining bright, we all played hide and seek.

Every night a coach arrived to take me to the ball.
We drove up through the starry night to reach the castle tall.
"The Kingdom's Royal Princess," I heard the herald call.

When I appeared the music stopped, I curtseyed to them all.
"Please everyone, don't make a fuss, I'm just a simple girl.
"With hair of gold and eyes of blue, and teeth as white as pearls."

"All my loyal subjects waltz throughout the night.
"Whirl and twirl until the dawn let every heart be light."

Handsome princes constantly were asking me to dance.
But I would look the other way, and not give them a chance.
My heart and all my kisses were always being saved,

For one gallant shining knight, the bravest of the brave.
He would come and call on me and ask me for a date.
"Come back," I said, "in twenty years. You see, I'm only eight."

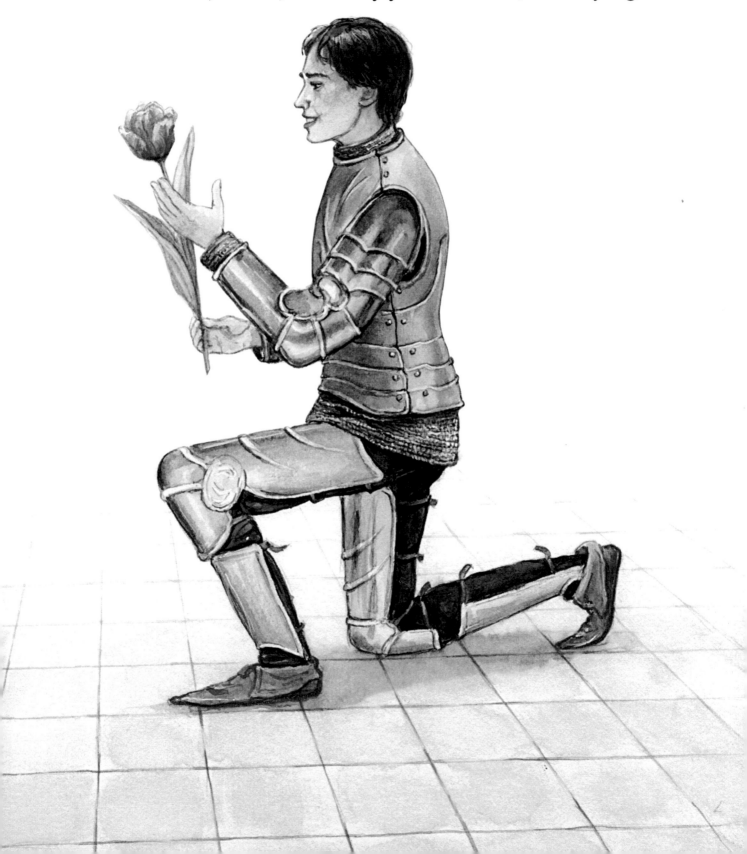

Then of course at midnight the clock would start to chime.
And I would rush away from there in just the nick of time.
My coach became a pumpkin or my mother's car.
And I was somehow taken from my dream so grand and far.

My mother's voice said, "Wake up dear, it's time to go to school."
Too quickly I was taken from the kingdom I had ruled.
I opened up my eyes to find myself inside my room.
My shining knight, my teddy bear, dressed up as a groom.

After school I climbed a tree and fell into a pond.
I came home covered up in mud, without a magic wand.
I was just my usual self, not hardly princess stuff.

My mother shook her head and said,
"Why must you play so rough?"
I washed and ate, I watched TV, I played with Mister Bear.
Bedtime came, I brushed my teeth and then I said my prayers.

Once again, I laid in bed awaiting slumber's bliss.
My father came to me and said "How was your day young miss?"
"Was there a boy chased after you and tried to steal a kiss?
"Tell them all that you're my girl, and I'll have none of this."

"Tell them that in twenty years, you'll welcome their caress.
"You'll let them take you to the ball, and wear your finest dress."

"But till then sweet dreams to you, I pray the Lord to bless.
He bent his head and gently to my brow his lips then pressed.
And just before - he turned the light - he said,
"Goodnight Princess."